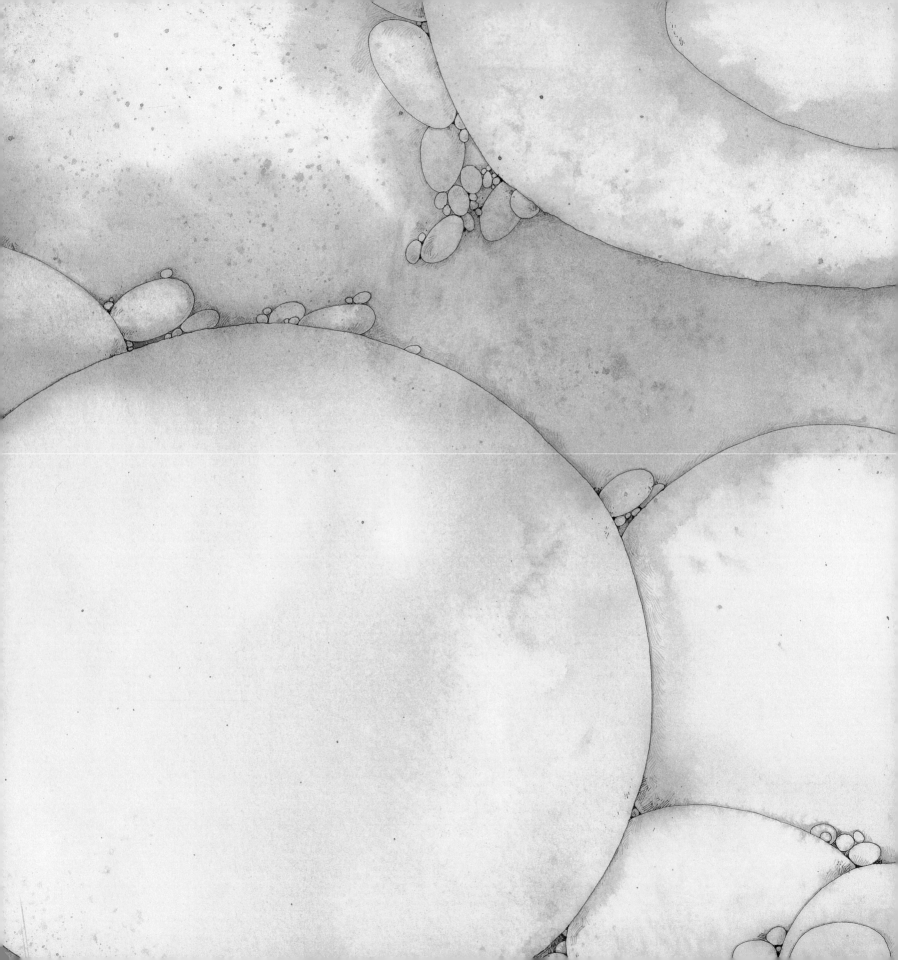

Wonderful
Life

For the dreamers who find themselves travelling further and more hopefully—

and for Sheila – H.W.

A TEMPLAR BOOK

First published in the UK in 2007 by Templar Publishing.
This softback edition published in the UK in 2008 by Templar Publishing,
an imprint of The Templar Company plc,
The Granary, North Street, Dorking, Surrey, RH4 1DN, UK
www.templarco.co.uk

First softback edition

ISBN 978-1-84011-349-5

Edited by A. J. Wood

Printed in Hong Kong

Helen Ward

Wonderful Life

Snutt the Ift

or

A Small but Significant Chapter in the Life of the Universe

templar publishing

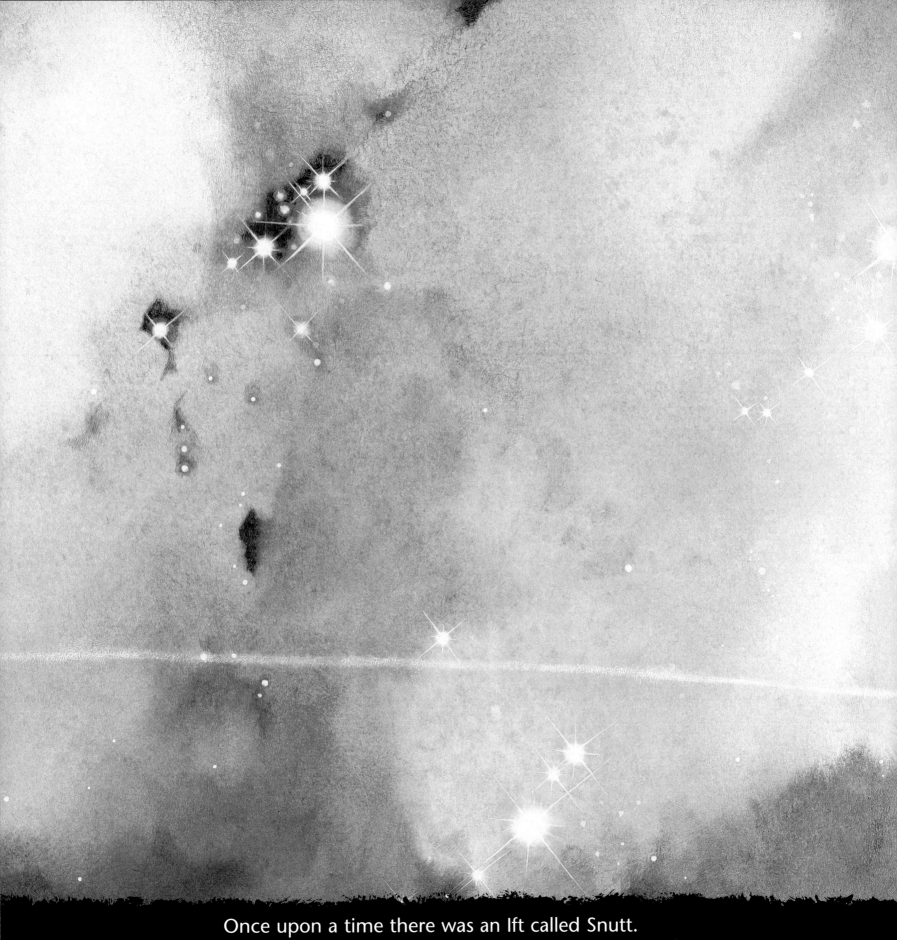

Once upon a time there was an Ift called Snutt.

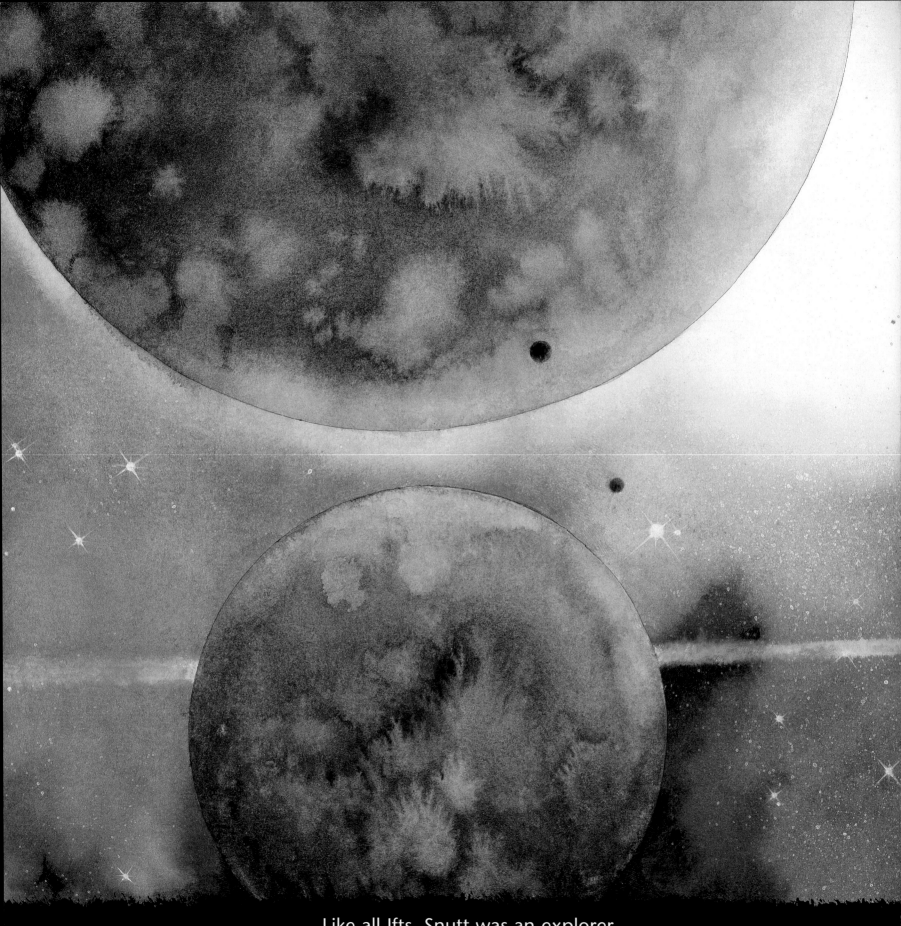

Like all Ifts, Snutt was an explorer.

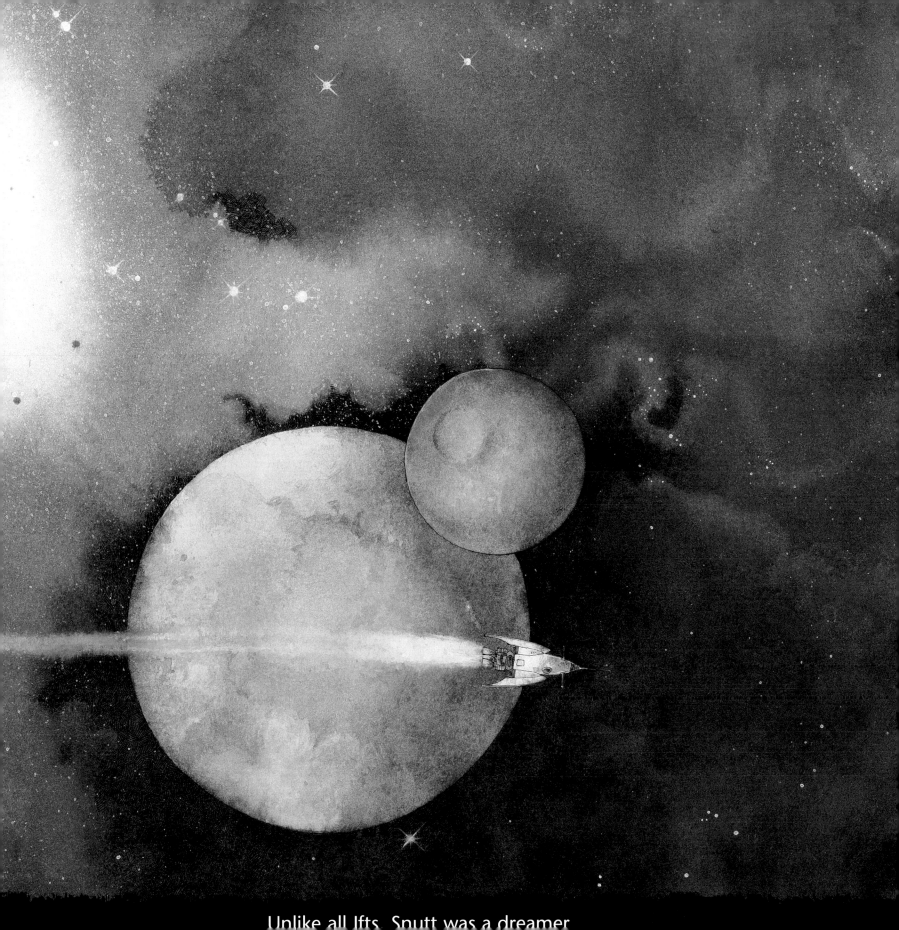

Unlike all Ifts, Snutt was a dreamer.

and for this reason Snutt travelled further, and more hopefully,

than any other lft.

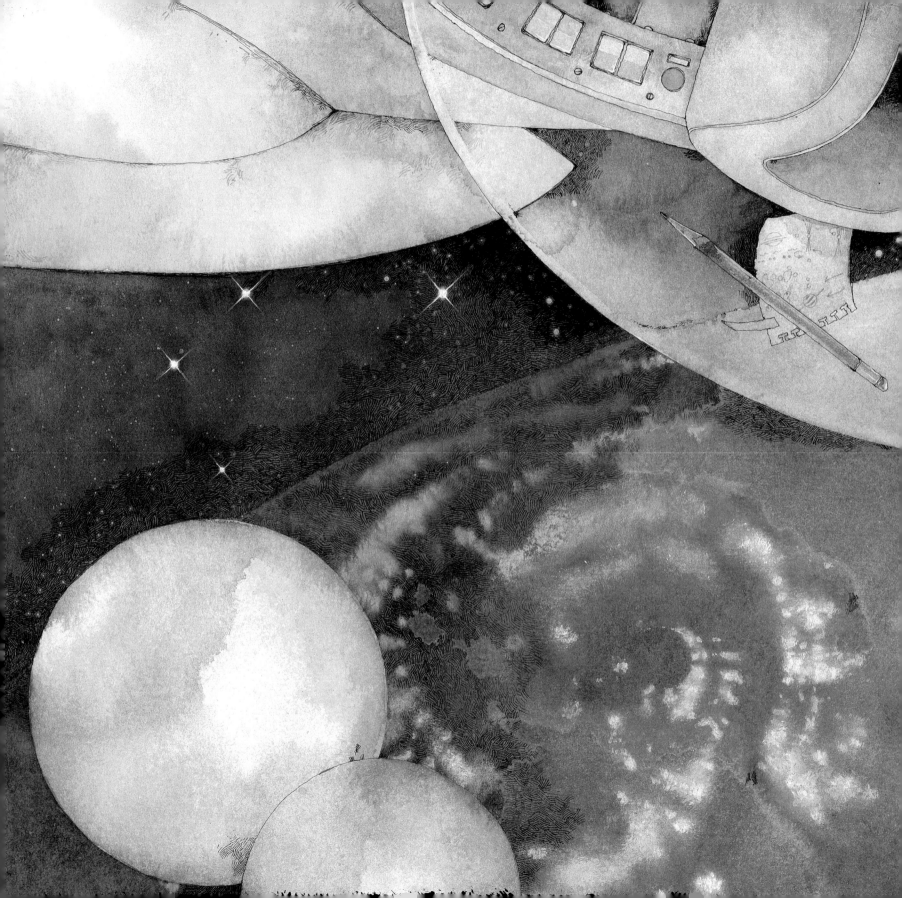

One day, Snutt found a wonderful planet.

A very wonderful planet,

with fields of cheerful tuffetills and delighted blossiblums

euphoric florifors and sticky-footed flewimols –

too flappy to make the usual notes,

too big to take the usual measurements,

too wonderful for the head of a lone Ift.

Suddenly and strangely,

and a long, long way from home, Snutt felt very, very lonely.

All the brilliant butterflings…

and fancy flewimols might as well have been dull grey dustmouts.

because Snutt had no one to share them with.

But this was, as has already been said, a wonderful planet

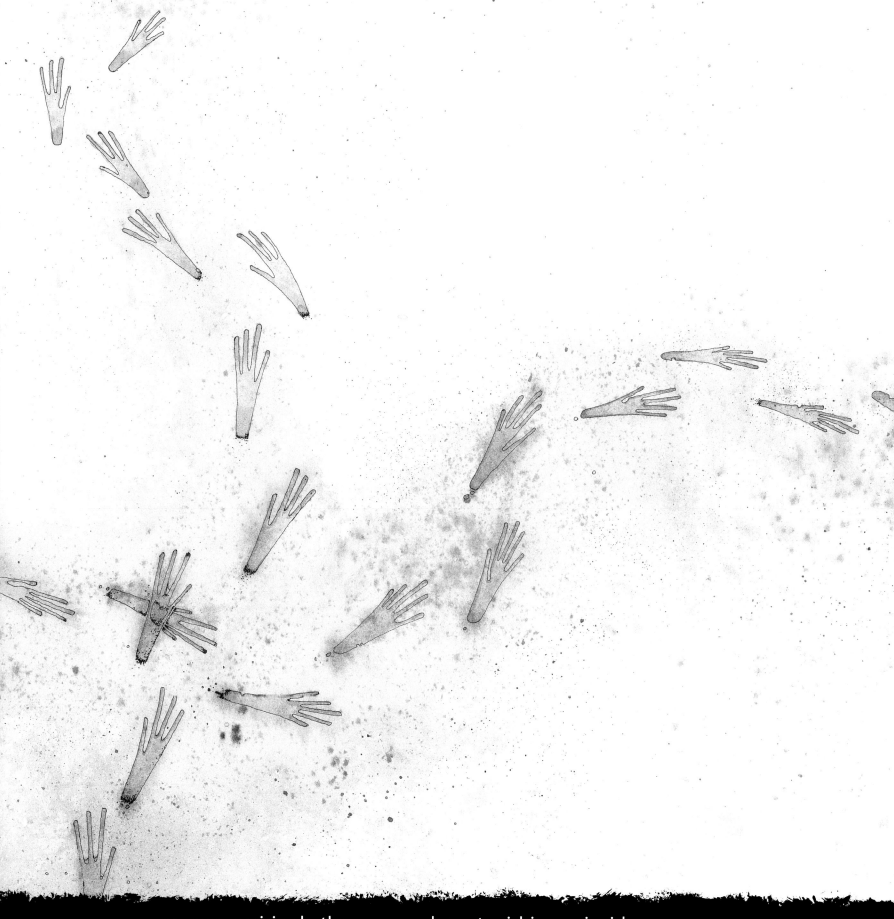

so, unsurprisingly there were also astonishing coincidences...

For Snutt was not the only explorer far from home.

There was also a Waft, lost for words and suddenly lonely.

The Ift and the Waft walked in almost the same direction

through the waving whishgrass. They oooed…

and they aahhed in almost the same way.

They listened and they watched.

And after they had found the very last amazing new thing

they looked at each other.

Snutt did what all Ifts do when they are very, very happy…

which was surprising…

but...

wonderful too…

like the universe and everything in it.